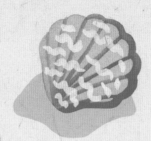

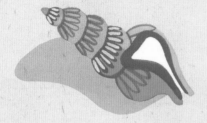

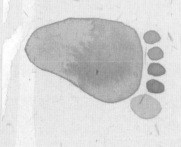

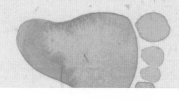
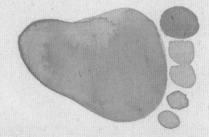

For Vince Reid, 1935–2001, one of the youngest
passengers who made that Windrush journey
J.A.

For the Windrush Generation
S.B.

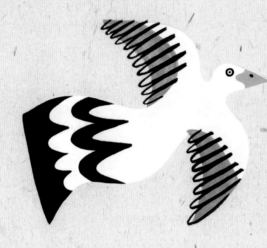

First published 2022 by Walker Books Ltd, 87 Vauxhall Walk, London SE11 5HJ

2 4 6 8 10 9 7 5 3 1

Text © 2002 John Agard
Illustrations © 2022 Sophie Bass

"Windrush Child" was first published by Walker Books in the anthology *Under the Moon & Over the Sea.*

The right of John Agard and Sophie Bass to be identified as author and illustrator respectively of this work
has been asserted by them in accordance with the Copyright, Designs and Patents Act 1988

This book has been typeset in Archer

Printed in China

British Library Cataloguing in Publication Data: a catalogue record for this book is available from the British Library

ISBN 978-1-5295-0112-4

www.walker.co.uk

JOHN AGARD'S
WINDRUSH
CHILD

John Agard

illustrated by
Sophie Bass

WALKER BOOKS
AND SUBSIDIARIES
LONDON • BOSTON • SYDNEY • AUCKLAND

Behind you

Windrush child

palm trees wave goodbye

above you

Windrush child

seabirds asking why

around you

Windrush child

blue water rolling by

beside you
Windrush child
your Windrush mum and dad

think of storytime yard
and mango mornings

and new beginnings

doors closing and opening

will things turn out right?

At least the ship will arrive

in midsummer light

and you Windrush child

think of Grandmother

telling you don't forget to write

and with one last hug

walk good walk good

and the sea's wheel carries on spinning

and from that place England

you tell her in a letter

of your Windrush adventure

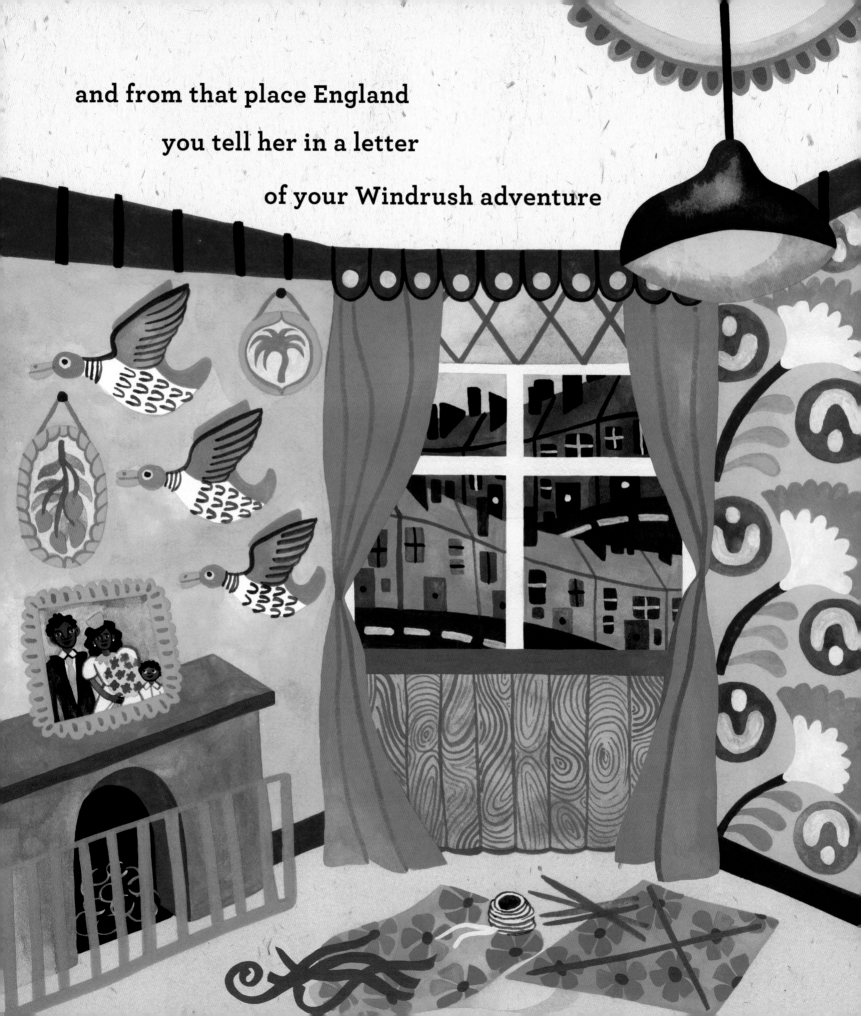

stepping in a big ship

not knowing how long the journey

or that you're stepping into history

bringing your Caribbean eye

to another horizon

Grandmother's words your shining beacon

learning how to fly

the kite of your dreams

in an English sky

Windrush child

walking good walking good

in a mind-opening

meeting of snow and sun

A Note from the Author

On 22 June 1948, the ship *Empire Windrush* arrived at Tilbury Docks, England. On board were hundreds of men, women and children from across the Caribbean who had paid the £28.10 shillings fee to sail to Britain. Among them were some famous faces, including the calypso musician Lord Kitchener, the jazz singer Mona Baptiste, and Sam King, who would go on to be elected Mayor of the London Borough of Southwark.

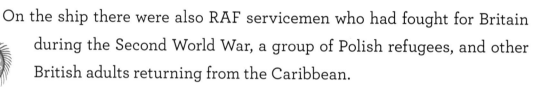

On the ship there were also RAF servicemen who had fought for Britain during the Second World War, a group of Polish refugees, and other British adults returning from the Caribbean.

Between 1948 and 1971, thousands of adults and children followed in their footsteps. These people have been called the Windrush Generation. Many decided to move to Britain as they hoped to make a new life. They were drawn by the promise of good jobs and opportunity from the British government, who had asked people in the Caribbean to help rebuild the country after the damage caused by the Second World War. Some were returning to Britain having lived here before or having fought for Britain during the war. Others came because it was an adventure. While some planned to stay in Britain for ever, others knew they wanted to return to the Caribbean one day.

When they arrived in Britain, they discovered a country that was different to their Caribbean home. It was sometimes hard to find jobs or even a safe place to live. But despite many challenges, including racism, they went on to build strong communities: friends were made, stories shared and unfairness challenged. Caribbean culture had a powerful and positive impact on British culture, and Britain is a much better place because of the Windrush Generation.

John Agard is a poet, playwright and short story writer who grew up in Guyana, where his love of language grew out of listening to cricket commentaries on the radio. He has won many prizes, including the Smarties Book Prize, the CLPE Award and the Queen's Gold Medal. He has been a writer-in-residence at the BBC, the South Bank and the National Maritime Museum, and he tours widely giving performances and speaking to students.

Sophie Bass is an illustrator of mixed British and Trinidadian heritage. She lives and works in London having completed her BA in Illustration at Falmouth University in 2013. Working largely within the music industry designing record covers, she has collaborated with musicians such as Yazz Ahmed, Soweto Kinch and Innov Gnawa. Her work draws inspiration from music, social justice, mythology and symbolism. Sophie works by hand employing traditional techniques with gouache and pen, to create contemporary images characterised by strong figures, vivid colours and a distinctive style.